The Book of Elsa

Dominique Hecq

PAPYRUS PUBLISHING
2000

Published by Papyrus Publishing
16 Grandview Crescent
PO Box 7144
Upper Ferntree Gully, Vic. 3156
Australia

Typesetting & Design by Papyrus Publishing
Front Cover based on *Deadalus' Daughter* by Amanda Wilson
Type: Titles—Elephant, Body—Garamond
Printed by Papyrus Publishing

This book is a work of fiction. The characters in this book are entirely imaginary and bear no relation to any living person. Although existing places and events are figured in the pages they are either the product of the author's imagination or are used fictitiously. Any resemblance to actual events or places or persons, living or dead, is coincidental and not intended by the author.

National Library of Australia Cataloguing-in-Publication entry:

    Hecq, Dominique, 1961-.

    The book of Elsa.

    Bibliography.
    ISBN 1 875934 29 4.

    I. Title.

A823.3

For Hena Maes-Jelinek
and for
Luke Murphy

Acknowledgements

My thanks are due to Claire Deliège, Beverley Farmer, Janet Frame, Marie-Thérèse Jensen, Hena Maes-Jelinek, Christine Pagnoulle, Judith Rodriguez, and Micheline Willems, all mentors of sorts whithout whom this book of fiction would not be.

In shaping the book of Elsa, I have drawn on a variety of texts. These are clearly identified as the stories unfold and every effort has been made to trace copyright holders. The author apologizes if any material has been included without permission and would be glad to be told of anyone who has not been consulted. Excerpts from *A Portrait of the Artist as a Young Man* and *Ulysses* reproduced with the kind permission of the Estate of James Joyce.

Because *The Book of Elsa* centres on a character who reinvents herself as an artist partly through immersing herself in a foreign language I wish to acknowledge my debt to those whose characteristic idioms I have appropriated. Special thanks to Paul for some very specific *breafkast* orders.

"Em*babelled*", the core section of this book, is a prize winning piece which originally appeared in bilingual form in *Writing (on) Short Stories*, Ulg. Press, Liège, Belgium. "The Hungry Lover" was published in *Kunapipi*.

Though perhaps a bit belatedly, I wish to thank Ann Murphy and Frederick Morgan for the use of the space above their workshop at Coomoora, where two of the sections from this book were drafted.

Thanks too to Amanda Wilson, for painting 'Dedalus' Daughter' as the whim took me, to Herbert and Clarissa Stein of Papyrus Publishing, and to my parents who, in funny ways, made this journey in other worlds and words, possible.

Finally, my thanks to David and Jerome for being such delightful babies when I needed to write to replenish my energy, to Emmanuel when the pressures of editing set in, and to Paul and Luke for making life worth living again when all seemed lost.

To be born is to come into the world
weighed down with strange gifts of the soul,
with enigmas and an inextinguishable sense of exile.

Ben Okri, *The Famished Road*

Contents

Prologue

Once upon a time there was, and there was not, a naughty little elf child who stopped listening and had to move away.

The elf moved away and dreamed about fathers, who did not have glazed green eyes flecked with brown, and about mothers who did not tell tales of venomous snakes or poisoned apples.

It was then that the elf who could not forget the sharp eyes of fathers, and the cutting tongues of mothers, realised that all dreams had died long ago.

At that she stopped dreaming, but, now, longed to run away, to a land as warm and colourful and weird as a hothouse, full of giant begonias, or circuses full of clever dogs with furry bonzes. A land of colours you could eat, like frosty blues and greens and deep purples and creamy oranges. A solid mass surrounded by dazzling waters, that land you could fly above and beyond at one single flap of wings. A land, that scorches and soothes, where the sun has many faces, and the wind brings few draughts but many whispers. Where sweethearts are aplenty, and fairy godmothers are bunyips. A land far far away. Further and farther away than fairylands.

One day—goodness only knows how, for elves cannot fly but only flutter like will-o'-the-wisp—the elf found herself in the Mirror World where the fairies are. And in that world she babbled and ran and prattled and danced and sang her head off, skipping and bouncing from one language to another, from one land to another, for she was racing Daedalus, her new father's father. When she sprang to her feet, one beautiful morning, it suddenly got into her head that she would beat them both at their own game.

At last, tired of running and dancing and chasing words and colours, and the colours of words that fly away and fall, the elf settled down in the land of furphies, sat down, and summoned me. For elves, unlike owls, do not cry.

One morning in spring I sat down with the elf. Under a huge wattle aglow, with a sun she called mother, and quivering in a breeze that sang of fathers you only read about in books.

I expected a long and tedious story told in a whingeing voice, but she did not utter a word. She stared at me until I thought that I would melt or fly adrift. She stared at me until I thought that she was only a shadow.

When I sneezed, she gave me a parcel that looked as though it had been wrapped in haste, or as though someone had tried to unwrap it unbeknown to others. In that parcel was a book—of course—a black ledger with a red spine and red corners and smooth yellow pages, the sort that you would use to record your diary or write your love poems or sketch your stories, but not to tear pages from.

Of course, yet at the time I wondered *why*.

Then I seemed to remember having given a friend a similar ledger, years and years ago, long before elves could tell, let alone write tales, a ledger, also crackling with scribbling: stories, perhaps.

—A labour of love, she had said.

To this day I do not know what she meant.

I took another hard look at the elf.

Like anyone else, I would have liked to have peered into her eyes, since it is said that the eyes are the mirror of the soul.

But this, I know, is not true. Besides, she kept her eyes shut tight, giving me only her large and protruding forehead to see. So white that I could hardly refrain from using it as a writing pad myself, and could certainly not help quoting some one else's words in my mind. *Azur*. So cold too. *Crisscross crisscross*.

Getting used to the twilight, I noticed the fine lines and stick figures drawn all over the elf's forehead.

Now allow me to say that a forehead is no easier to read than a pair of eyes. So I thanked the elf for her book and made tracks.

When at home I tried to remember my encounter with the elf in details so as to make a few notes about it all in my own notebook, I could barely see her in my mind, and I could not for the life of me recall anything that we might possibly have said. All I remembered was the sound of her voice with its vibrant intonations and colourful modulations. I kept this in mind, thinking it might add to my reading of a manuscript, the design of which already appealed to me. Inconspicuous enough, it was, but some of its features tickled my fancy: the reproduction of a painting at the very beginning, the engaging calligraphy, a folded piece of paper with a list of names, the plans of a dwelling traced in ink on rice paper, pressed flowers and four-clover leaves, more folded sheets of paper with stick figures and quaint patterns, bits of fabric and what I identified as a bundle of letters right at the heart of the ledger.

I was intrigued, to say the least; for the memory of another elf's sing song had made its way inside my ear as resolutely as the voice of a Pinocchio.

Embabelled

I am with those who know no words. They sit and stare and nod, in a no-time no-space. They twist their rings around their fingers. They do not see me. I twist golden chains around my neck, twist them around my index finger and tangle them, knot them. I: a knot of tarnished links in a net of no-time no-space.

They sit and stare and nod. They stare at the window pane. They stare at me. They know that others have propped up a scaffold around the old tower and they know that I long for some lost bower. But I, too, sit here and stare and nod for fear of tripping or blinking or slipping. I: a knot of stares in a crumbling tower.

One day I stumbled against the world. I fumbled for words and stumbled in here. The world tumbled. I tumbled down, and in, it tumbled over, and out, hauling my memory away. Now I stare through the window—past a eucalypt with leaves like tongues—at the world beyond: there is nothing out there.

Today a white uniform with a blank face looked at my record. I need some peace and quiet and a keyboard and a screen. I shall be moved to a private room with no windows, at the top of the stairs. I shall be taught how to use *Golden Words*

and Silver Silences. I shall retrace my steps and it will work.
I hear.

I have been through and down, and beyond, the tower of
hush and speak and hurt. I am back at the top. I have mastered *Golden Words and Silver Silences*, but I have not found
my way back into my *m*other tongue. There is too much
glitter, too much glare.
Sometimes I squint and look at the screen. Every time I see a
different chain of foreign words. Every time I recognise a
language I once knew, but there is nothing in it. My memory
is a glossy litter of lost letters.
I should print what I write, says the white uniform. I should
not be so stubborn. One should not desperately try to make
sense of what does not make sense. It would feel better if
someone read my words. The white uniform will read them,
or pass them on to some other.

*Il male di raccontare viene dal male di vivere: ogni evasione è
illusoria.*

Das Schwerste bleibt es doch, sich des Sprechens zu erinneren
und das Gehen neu zu lernen, um letzlich geboren zu werden.

ZE WAS MAAR EEN BABBELKOUS. ZE WAS ZICH VOLKOMEN BEWUST
VAN HAAR VERLANGEN OM WOORDEN TE LEREN EN VERHALEN TE
VERTELLEN, ÈN VAN HET GEVOEL DAT DIT ALLES BELACHELIJK WAS.
AL BIJ AL IS HAAR VERHAAL HET WANHOOPIGE VERHAAL VAN
VERLIES AAN ZEKERHEID : AAN HET EINDE WEET ZIJ ZICH ALS VROUW
EN MENS VOLKOMEN EENZAAM EN VERLANGT ZE ERNAAR IN EEN
TOREN OPGESLOTEN TE WORDEN.

Before the time of stories, men started to build a tower reaching up to the heavens, for they wanted to make a name for themselves and not be alone. God did not like this, as he could already see men living as one single people and speaking one single language. Thus God who not only saw the pride of men, but also knew his own fear, unnamed the culprits and discounted their tongue—and so was the tongue of men cut into bits that fit no lips and the tower of men left like a plundered tomb, and the multitude of men scattered over the whole face of the earth.

*And I was born cleft-lipped, and I am now starving here to death for words, em*babelled*. "FWhy? And who is the judge who called me out of my name and knotted my throat and walled me in and kicked me out and called me back Harelip?*

Nous brûlons de désir de trouver une assiette ferme, et une dernière base constante pour y édifier une tour qui s'élève à l'infini; mais tout notre fondement craque, et la terre s'ouvre jusqu'aux abîmes. (Pascal, Ed.)

I had not written for some time, so when the white uniform came in this morning and asked for a note and turned the computer back on, I thought hard.

I thought that it was strange how the languages I had learned came back to my mind in reverse order. I thought that it was even stranger that all I remembered in my mother tongue was but a quotation. I thought that this tongue must be dead, then, that it could not be dead but only tied. Then I thought how sweet it would feel to be disembabelled, and I typed in the only sentence I could think of. I printed the words in italics on a sheet of recycled paper and gave it to the white uniform. Who folded it without even glancing at the twisted letters on the page and then wrote something illegible on one of its blank faces.

I suddenly felt like checking something, but the uniform had gone.

I was up early the next morning: I wanted to tidy up the room and sort out the few papers I had kept before my daily encounter with my only visitor.

The white uniform came in at the usual time, with its usual face and countenance. I was told to sit down. I was hardly aware of the eyes peering into my face, the hand sticking a note inside mine, the voice explaining *the matter* to me.

My last notes had shown that the seriousness of my condition had been underestimated. This had called for a reappraisal of my case and it had been decided that I be referred to another institution.

I have kept the note I was given, and I re-read it every night before my bedtime walk, for it remains a riddle to my mind. One day it will all make sense.

THE PATIENT CLEARLY HAS FANTASIES OF DISEMBOWELMENT AND HENCE MUST BE TRANSFERRED TO ANOTHER UNIT.

I am now with Chris, my step-sister. I have my own room, with a view over her orchard, in her big rambling house. Chris is a wonderful gardener, a beautiful bread-maker, but a terrible house-keeper. She is absent-minded and never stops talking. She calls me *maestro*, and we play word games where she is my *impressario*, which means that she can be my confessor, tutor, editor, and censor all at once. Our tricks and pranks and words remain pretty light-hearted on the whole, and we try to keep the same roles, changing only the expressions of our faces, attitudes or voices.

One evening, though, after a supper, of goat cheese and heavy dark bread we had with plenty of Pinot Noir, she did hurt me. Not physically, of course. In fact she was so cool that there could not even have been an argument. She just told me how I freaked out the day she came to fetch me from what I insist on calling The Tower, how I yelled that I had no sister, and no brother, and no mother, and how I curled up in the corner of the windowless room. She also told me that I was my own and worst judge, and that, contrary to what I had said *and* written, I never retraced my steps, never even attempted to, that what I had been doing all along was pussy-footing around, hiding in my tower, becoming my own tower.

Today, Chris really lost her temper for the first time because I was nagging her about the computer. She gave me a notebook and a pen instead, or rather, she threw them at me. Before slamming the door shut, she said that she wanted me to be myself again and *cut the crap*. (So rude. Ed.)

Up to the age of seven, Elsa had been an impossible child. At home, she burst through doors, hurled her toys through rooms, held her breath until she turned blue and was often locked in her room to control her bad behaviour. At school, she got very good marks, but could never hold her tongue.

She also stole chalk from the teacher and fought with the other children who teased her that her father was a bad lawyer.

At the age of eight, her step-sister told her that everything would be all right if only she behaved herself. At this point, Elsa walked away from her life. She went inward and discovered the Mirror World. She has not come out since.

I am Marco, Elsa's right hand. I draw stick figures in my notebook, to illustrate Elsa's secret world which is a spiral inside a tower, and I write the mirror writing in which her diary is recorded.

I am Hans. I won a scholarship to study law. I trust no one and need no one, but people like my sense of humour. I help to protect the world from evil and evil from the world. I am like Elsa, or as she was as a student and believes her real father is. I look after Elsa's books as well as her health.

I am Connie, the good girl. I eat and speak very little. I want to be a teacher. I also want a baby, which disgusts everyone, so I take Elsa's cat as my baby. I am very lonely. Before going to sleep I imagine myself as Snow White, until I become as small as a pin and can see gold and silver stripes in my field of vision. Then I cry myself to sleep and I dream of making a home with my lover.

I am David, the tiniest and sweetest creature in the whole world. I live under the footpath and I follow Elsa everywhere. I am the only one who understands her *m*other tongue, and so we enjoy long secret conversations together. One day I want to translate Marco's mirror writing of Elsa's thoughts.

I am Esther, Elsa's twin-sister. I can move into Elsa's mirror world by twisting my head or by melting into the floor, yet I always watch the world from the other side of the mirror. I can see the colours of things, but I want to see *things*. When I was seven, I lost a little yellow dog, in the long green grass that was like water, near the church. I cried and cried and looked in the grass, but I saw nothing. Since then, I am green poison inside and my words poison other people. Now all I want is to buy back our family home and live there forever with a dog.

Chris is nowhere to be found tonight.

When I came back to my room, from a walk through paddocks boiled and bleached and scrubbed and beaten and spread out to dry in the sun whose virtues are vices here, I found my notebook open and my tower broken. I thought of that day, way back in the past and in another country when I stood still to devise my tower. A tower I dreamed about, of course, but which I later cut from a large sheet of glass, and the pieces I soldered together: opaque glass sections joined by lead, with a lid made of coloured glass fragments chained to the walls and with an interior floor cut in an old mirror speckled with rust.

And then I saw the reflection of the late August sunshine turn the leaves of the eucalypts into silver and gold at my mother's funeral.

Dedalus' Daughter

Heureux celui qui peut, d'une aile vigoureuse,
S'élancer vers les champs lumineux et sereins.

Charles Baudelaire, *Elévation*

In the Gallery of Mythic Art, in the Mirror World, hangs a painting by an anonymous artist, entitled *Dedalus' Daughter*. In the foreground at the left, a farmer is harvesting a strip of land next to a handful of youngsters who are picking grapes, whilst, at the right, a figure is carefully examining a *tundish*. The ridge beyond descends, past a flock of bodies in snorkelling gear, to a calm sea. The dim landscape in the background, with shreds of flaxen cloud here and there, and a tower at its centre, seems to be floating on the surface of the sea.

At first sight *Dedalus' Daughter* appears to depict an idyllic landscape, until you notice the outstretched arms of a figure drowning, or wrestling out of the sea, near the surfer at the lower right. This is Dedalus' daughter who escaped from her exile in the tower, on wings taken from a female eagle and fastened on to her arms with beeswax. Not wholly unaware of disobeying her father whom she was following in her flight, Dedalus' daughter flew too close to the sun for she could not help crying for the moon. Her wings melted and she plunged into, wallowed in for some time, then arose out of, what creative critics like myself call, the *m*other world.

This painting retells a well-known myth, of course; told and re-told through ages and spaces of histories. Take Ovid, for instance, who describes the flight of Daedalus and his son, suggesting that a fisherman and a peasant and a shepherd caught sight of them, and stood still in astonishment, believing that they were gods.

Here, too, despite the twist to the myth, the painter had Ovid in mind. This has in fact been pointed out by commentators here and beyond the seas. Mark my words. But what most seem to miss is that *Dedalus' Daughter* is also based on a famous painting by Bruegel the Elder: *The Fall of Icarus*.

What is striking about Bruegel's representation of the myth is that the three figures are unaware of, or insensitive to, Icarus' fate.

Now I would not have thought about it twice myself even though Connie, whom some of you might have met at the Babel Institute, had told me that the painting had nothing to do with the fate of Icarus as such but with the myth of the artist as exile. This of course was something that Elsa, the primary object of our curiosity, was ready to believe. Not being a Romantic at heart—God forbid, in these postmodern times!—though I am. Sorry. Cut this. That.

Anyway. I was however following all this a little more reserved and I read some books on, and around, the topic to make up my own mind.

> *Wings! Wings! they cried from all sides, even if we should fall into the sea.*[1]

Elsa later convinced me, when she showed me a poem by Auden, inspired by Bruegel's painting, which draws attention to this romantic theme, of the artist's isolation from life and society, in the final stanza. The poem is called 'Musée des Beaux Arts'.

Those lines gripped me at the time and have not released their grip since Elsa, who had so much insisted on signing the painting *Lucia*, erased the name, when the paint was still fresh.

We had had a terrible argument at the time and that is probably why she decided that the work should remain anonymous. But I have to confess here that Elsa is indeed the author of *Dedalus' Daughter* even though others helped.

The complex question of origin was—as you must certainly have guessed—the main cause of our rift, though there was also some disagreement about important aesthetic decisions. Thus Elsa drew a sketch of her subject. I improved the perspective and the architectural layout of the drawing. Finally Esther gave her advice on the selection of colours and Elsa, who had by then purchased a bigger canvas, proceeded with her oils. She used a lot more black and white than Esther would have liked. Black and white are values, not colours, and Esther only believes in using primary colours, for 'Colour is all', she says.

> *Colour is primarily Quality. Secondly, it is also Weight, for it has not only colour value but also brilliance. Thirdly, it is Measure, for besides Quality and Weight, it has limits, its area and its extent, all of which may be measured.*[2]

When we all looked at the half-completed piece, Connie annoyed us with her mock criticism in Dutch—translations of Dutch sayings and readings from the Bible—but now I can see that everything was linked. Since we only use English these days, except to express particular ways of thinking, feeling, and being, or what Elsa and Esther call *the wording of the world*, even our irritation or anxiety makes sense—because of our own contradictions, I guess.

Connie annoyed us, this is to put it mildly. Elsa was furious. She would prance around, repeating some of Connie's cheap comments, pursing her lips and scraping her throat:

ER HANGT EEN MISTIGE ATMOSFEER OVER HET LAND. DE VAL VAN ICARESS KAN EEN DIEPERE BEDOELING VERBERGEN. SOMS DENKEN WE DE SYMBOLEN TE RADEN, MAAR WE ZOUDEN ZE TOCH BETER WILLEN BEGRIJPEN. JUIST DAAROM WORDT HET SCHILDERIJ BOEIEND.

Then she would blow a few kisses to her imaginary audience and bow.

Elsa has never liked to be distracted from her passions and at that time her passion was the relationship between art and experience. I used to agree then with those critics who argued that what the anonymous artist had attempted to do was less to paint a variation on the theme of the myth of Icarus than to tell a contemporary life story in mythic terms. Now I understand that there was more to it than that, for the relation between art and experience, myth and truth, is reciprocal. *It works both ways.*

Elsa will never write an autobiography, perhaps because, like most autobiographies, hers would damage other lives, but mainly because all the significant elements of her life story are for everyone to see in this painting. As one critic put it, *Dedalus' Daughter* is a sort of mythical remaking. What is less obvious, of course, is that most, if not all, of Elsa's life is a mythical remaking where the same unrelated motifs become enmeshed. Or better, perhaps, as one viewer put it, *It's sort of naive mishmash so that it can speak to you.*

Thus, rather than attempting to lecture you on the many ways of reading this painting, I shall sit down and read out to you a brief account of Elsa's history. A putative *herstory*, so to speak, for it is my own translation of Elsa's painting. Please take one of the handouts stacked on the table next to the door if you wish to writerly-read the painting for yourself, later.

Elsa is the eldest of a pair of identical twins born at The Three Borders, a no-man's land between Belgium, Germany and the Netherlands. What Pina Q., Elsa's mother, was trying to hide, or hide from, no one knows, but what is certain is that she crept back home with a pair of twins whom she then had to formally adopt. This proved easier than expected, since these twins, born to a dark mother and fair father, were graced with red hair and slightly slanted blue eyes. They were thus registered in the name of the mother at one month of age. Although there was some toying with Christian names and other related question marks, the younger infant was called Esther and the elder Else. But because of a long history of linguistic feuds in Pina Q.'s own mother country, where cross-translating puzzles and myth-interpreting riddles are a favourite sport, Else was soon changed to Elsa.

As a child, Elsa never quite knew her place, and, as she has said on more than one occasion, was an *impossible child*. Although most children reach the age of reason at seven anywhere outside The Three Borders, it took Elsa one more year to become sensible.

Growing up seemed to take forever.

Chris, Elsa's step-sister was already twelve. She had done her first communion and confirmation. She was at boarding school, busy getting an education; she was learning a second language and music and ballet and *scientific* drawing. She wrote to Elsa, telling her she needed to be more *rational*—a word she had just looked up in her dictionary. She footnoted her letter, just in case, explaining what she meant: *Please, Elsa, do try to behave and it will be all right.*

That year, Elsa's mother packed a suitcase full of night-gowns and handkerchiefs and underwear and toiletries. One day at noon, she kissed everyone except Chris, who was away at school, and Elsa, who had no heart. She then shut the door on the twin with no heart and hopped into a Taxi that took her to the best hospital in the county.

When Elsa's mother came back from the hospital she was very weak, and so Elsa shut all the doors and windows, drew the curtains and the blinds, fetched more cushions and more tissues for her.

Elsa wanted to shrink to the size of a pin and disappear through a crack in the wooden floor. She kept still.

One day, coming down the stairs from her mother's bedroom, Elsa tripped and rolled onto the landing. She tried to silence the voice which said that she was a viper and a venom and a poison, but saw Connie in the mirror instead. At that, she went inward.

It was dark and tight, but there were soon sloping curves lined with mirrors. And so it seemed as though there was enough space and time for one, even two, three, four, five, lives; which was good, because her ever-absent father, who was always around looking, and watching and waiting to slash her throat with a shard of glass from his magnified eyes, would kill her again and again for being so deadly.

That night, Elsa had to sleep in the pigeon loft so that her bad behaviour could be mastered forever. That is when it all got mixed up in the Mirror World with its spiral inside the tower. She was Snow White sending kisses to the real world with the pigeons that were doves. Then, she was a dove, flying out and away and up to the skies. She was a princess trying out keys on locks in the tower of secrets, calling out to her sister who could see nothing but the green grass and dusty pathway outside. Then she was a tower made out of granite blocks that no one nor thing could break. The following morning she found out that she no longer knew whether she was being spoken to or through or from, so she bit her tongue.

The winter of the flood, she heard of a land where coral blossomed at the bottom of the sea, where swans were not pure and blameless white but mere trespass black, and where pure blacks like Friday could speak to fowl and fish and fickle fairies and fearsome explorers who spoke English. Then the Mirror World expanded and she was away. She was the vigil who was a bird who was the wind saying [land ahoj:] and [ankers awaj:] for she remembered those phrases from one adventure film with pirates and Errol *Fling*.

Oh, but when she found Chris's English dictionary, the world opened onto fabulous vistas. She started to learn words by heart: first at random, then methodically, starting with the letter —a. And thus she ventured into more and more fantastic landscapes and learned how to say ['trɛʒə 'aɪlənd ə'hɔɪ]. Space and Time sailing on surfaces, searing above, diving through worlds and words.

When she went to Chris's school, she had to get it all right. This took some undoing. Yet she was only too eager to bury her *m*other tongue with other dead tongues and to learn how to fit new and live ones into her mouth. Her mouth became a sieve and a thief all at once. Sifting through words alien to her mother tongue she found her father tongue and then her real father. But this was much later, in a story about a young man who yearns for some *mother* world and only finds the world of words.

In the meantime she mostly sat in her study. She read and drew and wrote and mused for lack of music, music being far too loud and resonant for secret worlds. She read the poems of a young woman who never left her father's estate, yet wrote of long journeys, through worlds of gossamer, into the realm of glowing light. Thus Elsa realised that whilst all thought that she had resigned herself to white windowless walls, she was, unlike her poet friend, perhaps, yearning for the light to lift her when the roof above her blew away.

And she was drawing captivity and flight and delight in the in-between.

She drew many sketches, hoping to paint a triptych in oils bearing the title of the middle painting *The Bird-Catcher*. So she drew dozens of studies and painted a few watercolours and oils, never being able to decide which to choose for *Birds of Paradise*, but fiddled a lot with *The Bird-Catcher*, who was in point of fact only a tiny hawk-like-figure in the background of the painting. She seemed to have spent most of her time drawing lyre birds and other birds of paradise—bringing out finer and finer details in ink on rough paper—or working on the feather sea which was deep purple and indigo stitched, with feathers for waves curling, in thick hard paint, scratched with sharp pens, dipped in shining black China ink, to make tiny flexible sticks like commas or accents, and with spots of emerald blue and white, for down, only here and there, to lighten up the picture. She had barely thought of *The Bird Seller*, then.

And as she went along towards some other world, at first further into the Mirror World, then away from it and far beyond, she discovered that many had taken similar paths. Somewhere along the way she recognised her father at the point in the book when he says *Away then: it is time to go...* with his own maker's voice saying

> *Yes; he would go. He could not strive against another....* Then of course, hearing in her own ears *I will not serve that in which I no longer believe... and I will try to express myself in some mode of life or art as freely as I can and as wholly as I can, using for my defence the only arms I allow myself to use - silence, exile, and cunning,* she was seduced.[3]

So what to do with it all but actually make the voyage?

Elsa was ready.

Now as light as a handful of feathers, she knew that she could soar through the skies, in the belly of one of those monstrous birds made of steel, without ever looking down, or back. Only twenty seven hours: three times nine hours to spare or waste before and after what it takes to dream or remember it all.

So she did.

So she did after the shame and hush and harm and sham.

But blunders damage and damage blunders.

A raft in flight she was.

And so she took the words of her farther, who was, and yet was not, to the letter.

And so she flew to the other side of the world as she had known it, secretly singing:

Silence. Exile. Cunning.

And all that she would choose too.

Of that period of her life we therefore know very little. There were a few stories, but mainly cryptic notes referring to being topsy-turvy in a land of furphies, or rolling down tossing hills, which suggests that she might have made a big mistake in choosing exile:

> *There was a bottomless pit: a tower inverted in jest.*
> And I sank in it.
> *Oh, but to scramble out of it.*

Elsa's father died during her first confinement. And so the news of his death did not reach her until it was too late to attend the funeral. Despite this, she carefully chose the words for an epitaph. Words that to her mind best described her father and her own kinship with him. Or in her own terms: *words that bound us and our worlds. Words like bandages, ages unbound.*

> Fabulous artificer, the hawklike man. You flew.
> Whereto? Newhaven - Dieppe, steerage passen-
> ger. Paris and back. Lapwing. Icarus. Pater, ait.
> Seabedabbled, weltering. Lapwing you are. Lap-
> wing he.[4]
>
> Your lapwing daughter Icaress

On the first anniversary of her father's death Elsa engraved the words she had chosen on a piece of frosted green glass.

Then she thought of a variation on her father's epitaph and engraved her own on indigo glass. Her father's, she sent with a wreath to Newhaven to have it affixed on his sepulture; hers, she tucked away in one of the jewel drawers of the vanity table next to the cradle in her fiction room.

M. D., Freelance Artificer
Open Air Lecture delivered at *Dis-moi*, All Souls Day 1995.

[1] Théophile Gauthier, *Histoire du Romantisme* (Paris: 1874), as quoted by Maurice Shroder in *Icarus: The Image of the Artist in French Romanticism* (Cambridge, Massachussets: Harvard University Press, 1964), p. 55.

[2] Paul Klee, *On Modern Art* (London: Faber & Faber, 1948), p. 23.

[3] James Joyce, *A Portrait of the Artist* (London: Grafton Book, 1977), pp. 221-22.

[4] James Joyce, *Ulysses*, (London: Random House, 1960), p.270.

Dear Elsa

Let the distance die, let time end;
desire for love becomes desire for death,
my other is my fellow,
my fellow is my other.

Edmond Ortigues, *Le discours et le symbole*

Elsa never liked her Christian name. Most people had a nick-name for her. I had a few: feather, snow, snow flake, moon and moon face, depending on our moods, I suppose. And some of the most vivid memories I have of our childhood is of her antics in the long grass between the pigeon loft and the church, where she used to recite lists of names, she liked better than her own, and mime the demeanour and actions of characters owning them. Names like Crescent, Devin, Eda, Musette, Rinah, and Thomasina, for instance. She would always end her performance with a *What e-else? Aah!* sung in a falsetto voice, then she would twirl around and bow before tip-toe-ing out of my sight, with her arms making loops in the air, elf-like.

When my father re-married I was already at boarding school, and so we saw very little of each other. She wrote, of course, but I never took much notice. I thought that she was making up a lot of the stories she was recounting in her long ram-bling letters, particularly about what was going on at home. I had a feeling that she was trying hard to sound clever, or win my sympathy.

But we grew up like ordinary kids and when the time came to leave home, we both decided to go to Australia. I had my reasons. She had hers. We left together, on a tourist visa, one freezing morning in January, then went our separate ways, all as expected. I went up North, determined to enjoy every bit of my *break*. But Elsa settled in Melbourne and soon managed to get a job at the Art Gallery, which surprised everyone. Perhaps she had pluck, after all.

Elsa's letters home, mum told me, were dull travelogues, or lists of *interesting people* she had met. Her letters to me, though perhaps more gossipy, contained very little about herself. They all were written to give the impression that she was happy about her life: she had become a free woman and a successful artist.

Then, one day, after a silence of several years, Elsa wrote again, telling me about the book she had written, but which had been rejected. She wanted me to read it. Could we meet, perhaps, and so forth. She described her book as *a spiral narrative in a mirror with anti-linear concerns*, adding, in brackets, *which is right*; for it *shows* some of the spaces between madness and creativity through the writings of many characters in one, or a catalogue of persons in the one person, who communicate with one another across micro-fissures, as in a brain, if you prefer'. I read through the rest of her exposition, not understanding much and frankly getting annoyed with her smarty pants ways. And in her last paragraph she complained:

> Except for one poet, no one has seen so far that my book is a sort of portrait of the artist as a woman, where the protagonist doesn't go mad but rather re-fashions her life in the light of the books she has read in a foreign language. Every-

one talks about subverting and disrupting received notions about writing or art or culture and what not, yet no one likes it when a writer plays with notions of genre and gender, voice and style, etc., not to elucidate anything or pontificate, but to *show* how it *might* well work (by 'it' I mean the unrepresentable or unspeakable disruption, or its eruption and implosion, explosion and resolution). That upsets me, for writing is all about subverting rules or surveying secret spaces!

She signed 'Feather' and then added in a long P.S.:

By making you more of an exile writing increases your sacred territory, pushes certain lines of flight to the point where it all becomes a dream machine, a sort of wordy *deus-ex-machina*, don't you think? Perhaps I'm becoming a bit too cryptic. But don't tell me that the book has no structure or that it's fragmented. It might appear so, but that's also what makes it all the more encompassing: it is full of correspondences with stuff we've read and fallen in love with—fairy-tales, poetry, lists of vocabulary, recipes, maps, novels, biographies, theories, you name it, or make it up. Think of Mallarmé (remember?) though Baudelaire and Rimbaud would do. And snap! Let go: allow yourself to be *mythtified*. Sorry, I just can't stop. You've got to get some things out of your system lest you remain out of step for the rest of your existence.

The day I finally decided to get hold of Elsa's manuscript I heard that she had disappeared mysteriously.

> Those things happen everyday, of course. But here, I was involved. And I felt guilty. I felt guilty because I knew that Elsa had always been frightened. Frightened of rejection, above all, which is not quite the same as not being loved. And in a way I had rejected her: I had hardly ever answered her letters. Besides I cannot say that I had ever cared that much about her work, which I knew was a poor substitute for affection, recognition, passion, or something of that kind. But I suspected that as she grew older and lonelier she must have become frightened of ending up in a mad-house. Perhaps, I thought at that point, she had had to write her way out of a knot.

But now that you are acquainted with some of the tales and characters involved in the story of Elsa's life, dear reader, you might like to make up your own mind. Perhaps you might even like to read the letters I found in Elsa's fiction room. These were tied, with a green satin ribbon, and tucked between two blank pages consolidated with cardboard at the centre of the black ledger with red corners. The letters are a certain Hans's undated letters to Elsa. I did not enjoy them much, but I decided to reproduce them here for two reasons.

First, there was a note, or a fragment of a note, in Elsa's handwriting on the top blank page:

Might be useful one day, if only to show what I
could (have) be(en) like.
Love thyself / thine self?
I must kill off Hans.

Secondly, I decided that a reading of these letters might recon-
struct part of the narrative around Elsa's departure, or various departures. Like my reconstruction, yours will entail a
piecing together of other stories of love and loss which form
the palimpsest of a secret life, as would indeed most letters
worth keeping. For one thing, such writing mercilessly cap-
tures the mean streak of unhappy lives and loves.

As Elsa's editor, I can only say that the letters make a broken
story which none the less sheds light on the main persona of
the Mirror World. This narrative also recasts some crucial
events in the plot of Elsa's life story. By stretching some hidden design out of shape it might thus be possible to release
for your private enjoyment the oft broken course of Elsa's
imagination and experience as well as fill the emptiness which
speaks through the cracks in Hans's words and Elsa's silences.
For, as you will see, evident here are not only the crooked
words of those who live and love poorly but also the rifts
through which what cannot be said speaks.

The quintessence of the book of Elsa is, I believe, here: in so
many *letters* with neither actual background nor action as such
to speak of, but moods, tones of voice, sentiments and attitudes. These surface with varying intensity or pitch and with
all the contradictions which are necessarily inherent in any
such essence of incongruous wholeness: the contradictions
which force decision of action on the stories collected, or rec-
ollected, here and elsewhere.

The letters themselves have neither been edited nor sorted out so as not to spoil the voice of the one or impair the ear of the other. I have preserved the oddities of the sender's style and spelling, and the order brought to the series by their first reader.

But lest I spoil your pleasure: Hark, reader! Look forward to the cult of uncertainty.

Dear Elsa,

I really didn't expect to hear from you again. I strongly feared
to have annoyed you too much by my last letter (your mixed
feelings?). Perhaps it's even a mistake to take up the pen again.
My mistake, then.

Well times have been changing. I left university after passing
the exams for the journalist school. The school is organised
by our biggest press-concern and takes one and a half years.
During this period you get a multifarious training including
practical work for newspapers and magazines (you'll never
get that same sense of being in the world working in your
area I guess). Trips abroad too. I was very lucky to pass the
exam: only 21 out of about 750 are admitted. I haven't decided about my academic career but during the last year I was
very dissatisfied about it. My professional aim is journalism
and now I've found a direct entry.

I haven't lost my interest in 'a room of my own', but I've lost
the time and energy due to my present occupation which is
very exhausting. All of my reading consists of newspapers,
magazines and technical literature. I am none the less still
reading Graham Greene. Greene is definitely fantastic: I like
his moods, the vivisecting and incisive observations. Love:
"Unhappiness was like a hungry animal waiting beside the
track for any victim." (A Burnt-out Case)

It seems that I have only been talking about myself, but how are you getting on? You will write me about your current projects, won't you?

Yours, still,

Hans

Liebling,

Thank you for your congratulations and all the rest. It was particularly nice to hear that you were taking your Dip. Ed. seriously and working hard.

One thing slightly annoyed me though: how can you say that you believe in me? Is it because it is easier than believing in yourself?

This is really a short note as I am packing my books and yours to go to London. Yes, back to square one, it seems, but this is an opportunity I could not possibly miss. I'll write to you about it when I get there if I can find the time. Perhaps we could meet somewhere in the U.K. as you were talking about visiting *Dedalus' country*. I hope that you will stick to your idea.

I really must go now.
Take care,

Hans

Dear Elsa,

Sorry for this long silence and thank you for keeping in touch. This has been the most exhausting and exhilarating year of my life, or, as you would say, *story* of my life. So much has happened that I don't know where to begin. I might send you a tape when Christmas and New Year celebrations are all over. But do you have a tape-recorder? You can be so old-fashioned sometimes.

You have already betrayed me your secret, your dream, but I am still wondering. You must be quite a contrast to that huge other land of bunyips and sunshine you long to visit, or am I simply caught in clichés? Remember the day you asked me to guess what music instrument you were learning and I answered — The violin, of course, because I thought that the violin was the perfect match for your temperament? Well, that is still the way I tend to think about people. So don't be annoyed.

The older I grow, the more I hate winter. Perhaps I am too much influenced by the seasons: I in summer, and winter, are two different beings. I wonder how I would fare in your country of bunyips!

With all my wishes for a happy new beginning then and that your own wishes may be fulfilled.

Hans

Liebkind,

Thank you very much for all your postcards and the news about your impending departure. It was lovely to hear from you after almost one year of silence, and I was pleased to hear that you had graduated so brilliantly. I must admit though that I was rather taken aback by the topic of your dissertation. I am glad to have withdrawn from journalism myself and to have enrolled in law.

By the way, to come back to your departure, my friends tell me that it might be cheaper to fly from London, as there are many companies competing against each other on that Sun Route, and there is even a chance that fares will come down even more if Mythic Airways are given permission to fly the route.

I am still working on my article on inter-textual law and am busy again at the moment as student officer. I enjoy it, because it gives me contact with expatriates and exiles and displaced persons and a few refugees, and I enjoy learning how the outcast tick. I shall resign at the end of this year, though, for one must move on. Actually, I am feeling quite refreshed after my two weeks' holiday. I had a very relaxing time, watching films on the video, tidying my files, dusting your books (I doubt that I shall ever read any of them), and catching up with friends from Switzerland, Germany and Denmark. Next

Christmas, I will be back in Zürich for at least a few weeks. It will then be three years since I have seen my parents, and I really miss them. You should think about this yourself.

This year Connie was with me in London. She did a second teacher training course in one of the Ozliz Schools in the city. It was a lovely year with her here. In August we went for a holiday together in Scotland. We were lucky because the weather was dry. We visited the Brontës' house in Haworth on the way. One of the nicest things was walking over the moors on Top Withins, the old farmhouse that is supposed to have been the inspiration for *Wuthering Heights*. — *A very Elsa thing to do*, said Connie, and we both laughed. But there was no running madly hither and thither nor any throwing up of arms to the sky nor even any quoting from the novel or from the best letters. Good and simple—or dignified—enjoyment of a good walk. Connie very much wanted to visit the Lake District, but that will be for another time, I am afraid. Scotland was very pleasant. We did the standard things, of course, but also revisited some of the places we saw with you the year before last. We did not go back to the Dominican Monastery, though, where you used to walk only to listen to Gregorian chants and chat with the novices, nor to the area around the docks where you used to roam at night or dawn just to see *real people* or get a glimpse of your damned *twylight*. Frankly, I sometimes wonder how you can still be alive, *poor suicidal Elsa* as Esther calls you.

Anyway, have you much further *work* to do before your departure? By the way, I would not take that art work or writing of yours, for that matter, too seriously. Sometimes I even

41

think that you might later regret having left not only your God and His Law but also your fatherland (or should I say mother country, perhaps?) and family as there is more to leaving one's past than mere word play. But never you mind, although it is now (sadly?) quite clear that we are already worlds apart I would still be interested to hear how you are getting on.

Best wishes with your passage.

Yours,

HD.

7, Greensborough Court
London
NWW 3PP
U.K.

Dear Elsa,

I hope that I haven't been disturbingly long in answering your last letters. As usual I have been snowed under with work. I have taken seminars for four weeks in the philosophy department again. Well, it means a healthy re-acquaintance with my favourite texts at least.

I am quite well, though I seem to be revisited by colds, far more often than I can bear, and suffering from overwork for the welfare of foreign students. A noble task, anyway.

I am getting a lot of fun following what you are doing in your new country. I hope your paper at the gallery of mythic art went well—although I was rather confused about who actually gave it! Or perhaps you are the one who is getting more and more confused. That outrageous story about the dead baby, for instance. As far as I know babies don't die of, how shall I put it, *lack of conversation*, perhaps. Your story about the experiment at the court of Russia did ring a bell though. But it is only a story, so don't try to match it by making ghastly incidents happen in your own life just to prove a silly theory. You worry me sometimes, you know.

By the way, do you know Vicky Swish? The niece of one of my acquaintances in Borgium who works at the Gallery of Mythic Art. She did write good poetry, but I fear that journalism will swallow her whole. But she will be a good journalist, no doubt, so what does it matter?

Cheers,

Hans

The Library
Borgium
N W S E O 1

Dear Elsa,

This will have to greet you back home I'm afraid, but I didn't have your letter in time to find you on our visit just before the new year.

Ah well! Here I am then, recovering from the Christmas break. As usual, we tended to rush from friend to friend, and miss many—but had a few happy accidents such as bumping into Esther at the cemetery in Newhaven. I looked for your father's grave to see whether the inscription you had devised had been properly placed, but I couldn't find it. I left it at that, though I could've checked at the Town Hall. But perhaps there is more than one place called Newhaven, after all. Did this ever cross your mind?

As you can see, I am writing to you from The Library of Mythtaken Books where I have been investigating a few matters related to what has now become my speciality (intertextual law in case you need a reminder). The stained glass window you used to rave about is, I think, still here, although it doesn't seem to correspond to your descriptions of it. I don't want to sound too disingenuous, but it did nothing for me—not shapely enough, perhaps. It may be that it doesn't represent anything anyway, but this is less a question for me than for your new friend Marco. I hope you will introduce him to me one day. I also looked for your translations and I found two of them. I was in fact very surprised to see that although the surname of the translator was yours, the Christian name was not! Why on earth would you use half a pseudonym? If it were a work of fiction, I could understand, but a translation!

By the way, I noticed that everyone here has a POETIC LICENCE sticker on the back of their cars, and couldn't help thinking of you. Here at least you wouldn't be out of place. Or would you? It's far worse than your 'Melbourne Roulette'.

I have heard from or of no-one at The Three Borders since I last saw you. Connie had a car crash after we parted from which she walked shaken but unscathed—a skid on water inside a tunnel. The other car was, as you might have expected, a *right-off*. Repaying her step-mother for the car is costing Connie her much treasured travel money, but she is working hard and with some help she might still make the trip back home that she has been planning so carefully for the end of the year.

Everyone else is doing as you would expect. I have no plans yet except for some underpaid work at the same student centre as last year, but I hope that may not be necessary.
I don't know when I'll be able to see you again, but may be you won't want to leave your *mirror world* anyway.

Have you forgiven me? Cheers,

Hans

The Gallery of Mythic Art
Borgium
N W S E 0 0 1 1

Dear Elsa,

I am glad that you have now given up all dreams of becoming a painter. I am not saying this to hurt you, but there are here so many good works that you would not have a chance. I know that you have joined the trendy clique of those who no longer believe in *good* and *bad* art or whatever, but as you can see, I stick to my guns. You do too, in a way—thanks for the *write-off*, but on the whole I think that this new country you persist in calling HOME has turned your head. Let me also remind you that not everybody is lucky enough to live in the country of their *father tongue* and hence continue to *steal* the words of others.

Perhaps you need a break, Elsa, although, what from I do not know, for you seem to be, how shall I say, a bit *at a loss* with those idle hands of yours. Or perhaps it is I who needs one. I am certainly deeply affected by this place and as you know I hate to lose control over things, so I tend to grope for old values and things again. I am terribly impatient with any form of nonsense. But anyway, I hope that we'll be on better terms next time.

I really must go now as I've just been packing the wherewithal for a walk on a wet wintry day. Whether I shall return, woebegone, to the library within an hour, only time will tell.

Kind regards,

Hans

PS: I wish you would not say things like *bashing the keyboard*.

Dear Elsa,

I am returning to you here the *translation of a drawing of one of your rhyming thoughts by Marco*, as I am sure that you sent it to me on impulse and will find all this embarrassing one day.

Although you did not ask for my opinion in so many words, it is clear from your letter that you wished me to comment on your piece. I do not mean to sound harsh, but to tell you the truth, I found it both pretentious and self-indulgent. Without the epigraph, perhaps, and with less ethereal words, if you excuse the lack of linguistic precision, it could pass for a little playful romantic lyric. It is not, however, a poem as such.

Why do you persist in trying to write, if I may ask? I do not believe you when you say that you write for yourself. Everyone speaks or writes for an audience. Frankly, I think that you should stop to fool yourself, for I don't think that your command of (any) language is good enough. Perhaps if you had perfected your mother tongue, instead of learning all these languages and ending up not speaking any properly you might have achieved something. But I am afraid that you have wasted your energy and lost your best chance. Anyone can tell that your English is unnatural, your Dutch school Dutch, your German unpalatable, your Italian practically non-existent and your French, well, pathetic. So, *Why bother, my dear?* as that

47

darling old lady you used to stay with in Gippsland would say. There are far too many writers in the world as it is. Very few are good, though. And *why bother* if you are not excellent? Why, do you think, do I want to become a lawyer? I who had been praised and pressed so often by the very author of *Das Leben des Klagenden Faustus*? But you should know my views on the matter by now.

This brings me to another point prompted by some remarks you make in your letter. I should very much like to stress that madness is not a precondition to art, although it is true that a lot of artists are mad, or sick people with delusions which appeal to the public.

To conclude this letter, I would advise you to pull yourself together again if you can, or else seek therapy with a psychiatrist (I would discourage you from using any psychoanalysts, particularly those who indulge too much the patient's pathological dependence on language). I include the card of one of the best oncologists in case you decide to make an effort of will power. It seems to me though, that the likelihood of your having contracted leukaemia is part of a broader, albeit less serious, *maladie imaginaire* to me. Yet that would be by far the best alternative.

Trusting that you will regain some dignity, here are the details of Dr Swish as from last week:

Dr Adam Swish
Department of Honkology
Bloomington Road

Krankville
Borgium
Tel. (040) 78 84 82
Fac. (040) 78 87 22
Email. Honk@cryptic.rch.uniborg.edu.mir.

Mit meinen besten Grüssen,

Hans

Rhyming Song in Fall

Zénon! Cruel Zénon! Zénon d'Elée!
M'as-tu percé de cette flèche ailée,
Qui vibre, vole et qui ne vole pas!

Le cimetière marin.

It was your smile, came and rent
all I meant-
all that vermeil and argent
filtered down with heavy scent,
so it found vent-
all that I meant, roused & rent.

It was your smile's true accent
in all I meant-
gently-formed and heaven-sent,
of intellect and feeling blent.
Outward and on it went-
all my bent, true accent-
ed new intent
I trustingly
upon the winds unbent.

Icar(el)ess, Fall 1987

The Hungry Lover

La langue de la vie nous fondait dans la bouche

Paul Eluard, *Tout est sauvé*

A silhouette slipped through the orange-blue heat of an early summer evening and melted in a bower swollen to the point of bursting with vine leaves and unripe fruit and the gossamer discarded by caterpillars.

Hands put down a large tray on a dinky table spread with long streaks of sunset.

She sat down on one of the golden chairs with an erect back, that reminded her of some ever absent, ever present, guest silently waiting for champagne to be poured. She sat and crossed her legs. Replete with sunlight, she glowed like an elf at dusk and waited—for waiting now seemed to be the answer to it all.

A long time ago, when she used to fancy herself as a natural dancer and painter who could reinvent the wording of the world, she had waited for eternity, seeing herself as a vigil who was a bird about to take flight or a gust of wind carrying messages of hope and oaths. Now she was a vigil beaten by the sun on a dead sea, convinced that horizons melt into mirrors or shrink to naughts, yet longing to drift along with some vessel, were the breeze about to whisper.

She heard the rolling and rasping and crunching of the gravel, the snoring and gasping of the motorcar. She saw him in her mind. He stood hidden behind the thick veil of greens and greys, eating her up with his eyes, then spitting the bones in disgust.

Gone were the days when she could have killed for love, she thought. And she checked herself. Whole and hollow, like a bubble of molten glass that will not burst.

Since she had recovered her childhood figure, she knew that her mouth always repelled him a little, with its look of dried shell gnawed off by time starved for void. Even *she* hated to look at the lip-brush in the mirror, hacking at her mouth— with the lip-gloss never wholly covering the wound, and the lip-liner, sucking flesh from chin to cheekbone, making her look like a famished hare. Yet seeing now more clearly in her mind the smile she had managed to sculpt in Pink Pearl Bourgeois lipstick, she felt a bit better. This surprised her, for though she knew that she was not quite past wanting, she had hoped to be past feeling.

As long as she could remember she had starved for something: freedom, love, knowledge, her *passions*, but also words as flat and drained as old flabby breasts. And so starvation had brought only starvation.

Now she could see this, but it was too late. Her end would never be her beginning, nor anyone else's, for that matter; for the wounds she had inflicted on herself and on others with her *sigh-lances* were festering with unspeakable hatred— you don't *lose* a child *just like that*. The scales had tipped, subtly: the void was starving for time and time for her.

Her *Eternity*.

Molly, a godmother after her own heart, would never have starved, she thought. Molly had pluck. She married twice. There were stories of passions and poison and puzzles. When Molly found out that no child would come out of her first marriage she poisoned her husband. Then when Pina, her daughter, wept over a set of unnatural twins, Molly told her all about prickly pears and how their furry prickles can stab the hearts of culprits unawares. The father of the twins died in his sleep shortly afterwards. He died of natural causes: a heart-attack.

She looked at her sleeveless black cotton lace cardigan with gilded buttons and heart-shaped neck, her filmy yellow gazar skirt with Andalusian spots, and her jet black suede pumps. She slipped her sharp knees and smooth calves away from the shade underneath the fabric, rounded her chest in the lace and gestured her slim arms and fingers into life. She laid her nails of pearl on the Andalusian spots and looked at her thin wedding ring.

Still. Heart chilled. Memory roaming about.

Dim memories of the Northern hemisphere. Bright memories of longing to leave.

How ridiculous!

She must have hated him all along, she thought, for now she could see that she had borne the essence of her birthplace inside her throughout the story of her life. This, of course, she shared with those who talked about the burden of being born, which is not quite the same. The essence of her birthplace: the three borders fencing in the kingdom of boredom. Lack of air, lack of warmth, lack of sound. A fiefdom where all dreaming was of storms and heat and clamour. Dreaming fierce as fighting.

He will bring a bottle of champagne to celebrate the occasion, of course. Seven years of married life, away from home that was never home until all hope of making one dropped in the pit. A barren marriage. Ha! She could remember nothing of the wedding. There were photos, of course: a timely recording of fleeting instants of make-believe. These must be burned, she decided, now that all love was dead, now that there only remained the love of death. The utter fascination.

— Champagne?

— Not Veuve Cliquot, please.

That vow which almost took shape, that child who crumpled back to nothing before being fully fleshed out, that love which crumbled, turning a desire that never was to dead matter. Desire to be born and to be still.

Her fingers slipped on the Andalusian spots and she felt the only roundness on her body since she had been with child. And she remembered her delight in fasting—a compulsory fast meant to bring new life. But then she was not sure. For there had been the other fast—as if fasting could ever have given any life back. Or buried one perhaps and many mishaps in the same pit. Or covered the guilt and shame with the same blanket. Where had she been? For she did remember the newspaper headlines : INFANT SMOTHERED AT THE BREAST and then, of course, *The Lethal Breast*, the book he had given her. She never found the courage to read it. A pity, perhaps.

But why always *the breast*?

It is the womb which is a tomb.

This she will have to think about.

She now revelled in her weightlessness.

Pop! went the cork. And he, in the claret-orange light with a bottle of *Veuve Cliquot* in his big white hand, with its thick golden ring, filled two glasses with golden bubbles, then placed a dry kiss on her parched forehead.

Champagne flowing again, but words, no.

His eyes were hungry, it seemed, devouring the shape of her body, yet far from feasting on it. His, was a nasty kind of hunger.

— Cheers!

And he uncovered his teeth, like a dog about to growl.

She thought of her first love. Or rather, the ending of her first love story.

She had just moved into a rented flat on the third floor of a seedy block of flats in *Little Firenze*, a swish area of the suburb of Carlton, near the mosque, which she re-named after the glorious view over waves of terracotta and skeins of green from the North window of her Tower of Rest. He was downstairs in the drive, changing over the starter motor of his clapped out Austin and chatting with his *mate*. She was enjoying whiffs of fresh breeze, watching them, catching bits of conversation.

When she saw them hop into his car, she knew that here was the end of more than one affair.

He wound his window down and shouted to her to get them a cut lunch ready as they were both off to the beach for a picnic. She laughed and shouted that what he needed was not a lover, but a dog. And she shut the window on his snapping, *The bitch*.

They drove off.

She packed her things and left.

The following weekend she came back and let herself in with a blue healer on the leash while he was playing tennis. She went into the bedroom and dragged her patchwork quilt from under the bed. She left the dog asleep on the quilt on the bed with a note saying *Here is a proper bitch for you*.

The mangoes were a screaming yellow and the wild rice black as death. But the rest of her spread had lost all appeal. The salmon was a mere shade of bronze with smudges of laminated pink, the asparagus a mess of green and dirty purple and the avocadoes had turned the colour of wet ash.

She felt sick.

One mouthful and she put down her knife and fork.

He stopped eating too.

They each looked into the distance. Past each other.

Her knife and fork were all glitter on the table and flickering tongues of fire on her face.

Already far away, she did not answer the question she had not heard.

She was way back in time. Back to when they first devised the house they had built together—a silly design, meant to accommodate all of their needs and dreams. The topsy-turvy tower had been her idea, this is true, she had wanted a place where North and South, day and night, past and future, would collapse into one another in a space she had hoped to call home one day. And so they took the Jethro Coffin House, they had visited at Nantucket, and an old Flemish windmill, and merged them together. The result was a weatherboard high-gabled but long rambling box for the use of *the family*, with, at the back, a windmill tower merged into a lighthouse for her own use. There had been talks about installing glass solar panels on the house and removable sails on the cap of the mill, but nothing had ever been done about this. She had left the top of the tower unfurnished to hang her old photographs and new paintings on white-washed walls, and she had turned the ground floor into a studio. But all of her paints and brushes and soldering material, all of her glass collection and all of her books and papers and half-written pieces had remained packed in fruit boxes along the walls of her tower for years now, together with her drawings of sails with the cloth in curled position, sword point, dagger point, and full sail position. Yes, in that order, she thought.

At this, her wedding-ring seemed to loosen its grip on her middle finger.

She got up, threw her knife and fork and yellow napkin with lilac flowers on the white-washed lawn and rushed to the house.

He had got in first. He stood in front of the bathroom mirror, ready to catch her shadow. She stopped for a minute, watching this mask, his face, in the mirror, then went straight to the mahogany vanity table. She felt his gaze turning her flesh to gauze, ripping it, reaching for her bones. She got hold of a bottle and shook it; she unscrewed the top and dropped two green pills in her hand.

Hands.

But these were no longer hers.

The bottle smashed on the bathroom floor. The pills rolled and bounced on a bed of broken glass.

Glass.

Like her body: transparent and cracked. All broken inside.

She held her breath.

A jar with purple tablets shattered at her feet. SVELTESSE knocked the edge of the bath and spilled on the carpet. BIOPHILE flew into the toilet bowl. FORMYLINE crushed under his foot. Some appetite suppressant mixture was already swelling in the basin where bran tablets were melting away. Blue, yellow, red capsules: a shower of primary colours for prime labels. LUMINEUSE, CORFIT, LIGHT, CORFOU. Gone. All gone in the vandal-proof stainless steel bowl designed for prisons.

— Leave me alone, she screamed. You self-righteous bastard. You... You understand nothing! You pontificating prick. You f... You. I hate you.

— I love you.

Three days and three nights swollen with silence rolled by. Unbearable swellings of time. Seconds. Minutes. Hours. Days. Bloated days and puffy hours and puffed up minutes and bulging seconds. All ready to burst under the sharp point of sorrow.

A blue-orange breeze blew in cool gusts through the bower. A shape all curled up under the veil of vine leaves shivered. Arms came untied, legs unlaced, and like an elf brought to life in the space of an eclipse of time she left her shelter of faded light.

She found him in the kitchen.

He sat on a stool with his head in his hands, staring at the cover of *The Hunger Artists*. With his back arched, he looked frozen and about to break. He, too, had had his fill of the insatiable lack of appetite.

A noise.

A word, perhaps.

His spine, shoulders, neck, and face relaxed. He glanced at the silhouette in the doorway.

—I'll give it a go, she said, taking a few steps forward.

She stopped and looked at his face: splashes of cream and pink on grey.

She shut the door and leaned against it.

He got up, went to the dresser, paused and twisted his head around. He stepped back and took the slide-tray out from underneath the butcher's block and put it on the table. He got one knife and one fork out of the drawer, one white plate from the plate rack, then a bunch of red grapes, an avocado and a mango from the fruit bowl. He put the fruit on the tray, not even bothering to lock the castors.

Then in the manner of inexperienced lovers, nervously trying to impress, he placed the tray on his fingertips and brought it back to the table while still feeling for the point of balance.

They both sat down at the table, carefully, poised as they were between their starved yet ever unnamed desires.

She waited, watching him peel and slice the mango and avocado pear, then arrange the perfectly proportioned segments of fruit in a dual arc of colours around a cluster of grapes on the now translucent white plate.

As though soothed by the colours of these late summer fruits, they started to eat, with him feeding her. First one piece of avocado, then a second, and a third one. She crossed her hands, and he looked at the orange monochrome absorbed by the mango peel. He had a cube of the fruit, taking his time, as if looking for the answer to some riddle in the rich and tasty flesh. He took a second cube of mango with the tip of his fingers and offered it to her. She chewed it slowly, trying to recapture the complexity of some forgotten flavour. He fed her another piece, and yet another, then a grape, opening his mouth in imitation every time she closed her lips on a cube of orange, on a bubble of dark purple.

— There's something missing, she said.

— Not your wings again?

— No, that's for later. What we need now ... I mean, is to feast on words.

The City Post-Partum

My swirling wants. Your frozen lips.
The grammar turned and attacked me.

Adrienne Rich
A Valediction Forbidding Mourning

In the resounding *twilight* I am free; for my mother, who was
many, took the life and the voice out of me.

I am as big as a drawing pin and as heavy as fine dust dancing
in the early morning sunshine. I am made of the down of lyre
bird, but my eyes are those of a hawk and the lining of my
throat is that of Flaubert's parrot. The silk of my body is
soaked in precious duck oil to protect me from the whiffs of
evil winds. My heart is that of an eagle owl, but my mouth
holds it with soft lips, not the hard mandibles of birds of prey
or passage or paradise. And because my feet are cut in the
scapulars of a bittern, I have only one passion: travels.

I once took a holiday between Christmas and New Year in a
bunyip's cavernous nose. A wicked place for a holiday, a
bunyip's nose. It is like a monstrous honey comb, whose cells,
as you go further inside, are crammed with treasures like li-
ons and skulls etched in grains of sand, letters printed in flecks
of gold found in the beds of dormant creeks, and sighs tin-
kling like specks of silver in the late spring breeze.

Not long ago, I stayed at an elf's den. I had met the elf at a
midwinter party where Stephen Dedalus and Icarus were
drinking wine with Charles Beaudelaire. Because the elf liked
my stories about mother, she invited me back. And so for
days on end we made bread with grains of wheat and corn

and rye stolen from fields bordering her no-man's land. Bread as fluffy and fuzzy as fairy floss. One day at dawn, we made butter with the milk the cat had spilled on the mat. The same day at dusk, we stuffed mosquitoes to give to the frog to fry. And we sang songs telling of farmers who eat bacon and eggs for *breafkast*. After that last hard day's work, when all of a sudden the den turned into a glowing opal, I agreed to moonbathe on one of the elf's large toenails. It all shone like pearls just fished out from deep waters as offerings to either moon or sun, or both, in midsummer.

I also remember spending some time at a Ha'Hem, with a yobbess who used to preach to midgets. She was then in the prime of her life. She had become tired of preaching to creatures who knew no better than mocking her ways and had bought a piece of land where she had a Yobhus built. When ready to move into the North wing of the mansion, she ordered a few varieties of worms to prepare her soil and time-proof her shelves. She then invested the rest of her money in a word farm. Many could not, and still cannot, believe how she became a legend of fame and wealth at one single stroke of the pen. Yet she can now afford to while away the time indoors, idling amongst her impressive collection of coloured glass fragments and fragments of one mirror inherited from a vain queen, retelling the tale which fostered many *herstories*, including the tale of her own story.

The best spot for a vacation though is perhaps a castle in the air. I stayed in one a long time ago, with my mother who was then rehearsing for a baroque concert. It was fabulous, for the ghost of my great-grandfather lives there. He is Daedalus and tells wonderful stories about his own country. He and I had a great time building miniature castles with blocks of breath caught from mother's singing. One day I want to go back there and work hard on my own breathing. Then I might recover my voice and even learn how to sing.

Most of the time though, I am under the footpath and I follow mother everywhere, crawling head down, holding on to the underside of stepping stones with the unmatched barbs on the soles of my feet. Except at night, of course, which is a bottomless pit of time lost to spirits. That's when wandering around is most exciting.

Although it is always damp in here, I can not say that I ever feel either cold or clammy. Not only do I have no sense of what is hot or cold, wet or dry, I do not feel the need to check my own pulse all the time. Nor say things for that matter, since words, which are my food, are put into my mouth at regular intervals.

Mother, who has lost all sense of taste, feeds me. But she tries to give me only words from her own tongue: this is rather tricky, as her tongue has been infected for some time. *Multilingual thrush*, a famous physio-linguist called it the day I first met him at The Babel Institute. It is worse than what it sounds. Not only is the affected area covered in white patches with raw sores underneath, it is also riddled with tiny holes, so that the fungus reaches far beneath the surface. These holes are caused by trash, which is an *intra-* rather than *inter*lingua phenomenon. A real pest. Mother's condition is thus best described as a *sub*version of plain lingual thrush.

And so even if it sounds as though we are chatting incessantly, she is in fact talking to herself all the time. *It is like speaking a foreign language*, she often complains around midnight, when drunks are leap-walking, and she, falling asleep.

I, on the other hand, do not need to sleep.

Thus I hop and skip and run under the footpath with mother

guiding me all day long through the Mirror World only to pop out at dark for a visit to the city of the departed.

Now

This is a good spot. For the space between the wooden bricks that survive between tram tracks is huge here and I can use the grain of the wood as you would steps.
Follow me, it is unreal.
Simply magic.

Out there, two miles or so South West, is my favourite spot: that great big building which looks soaked in gold now with the rain and electric light splashing on its yellow walls, dripping and dribbling down into the guts of the city. That is where my first memories of the twilight world are. Or that is where I saw the *twylight* for the first time and learned about *forgetteries*.

It is always best to get in through one of the back doors on level one.
Now, let's hurry past the sign that says CASUAL. Past the woman holding a baby, and past Anon who is dangling his legs down the couch, looking at the woman who can only see inside herself whilst staring him hard in the eyes. Past the lady in a sari. And past the family of four waiting for the lift. Past the gentleman in a navy suit who is leaning on the desk. And past that big colourful board with signs meant to confuse visitors.
There is another lift around the corner.

Out this way.

And in through this glass door.

I can see Mickey Mouse and Minnie Mouse and Pluto and Donald Duck amongst a handful of children, some in party clothes, others in tracksuits, or in pyjamas, and even one in plaster, it seems.

Mickey and Minnie are holding hands, trying to make eye contact with a tall and skinny boy of eight or so.

Pluto is creeping behind twins with red shoes and red ribbons in their fair hair, muzzle down and bottom up, muzzle up and bottom down. Yap yap. Yap yap.

And Donald is wooing a teenage girl with a thick and stiff collar around her neck. She does not care and runs away. Kwack kwack. She will be back.

Donald Duck's sweetheart is eating a pie out of a paper plate that does not even look like a plate. It is *today's special*: heart and liver and gizzard and giblets pie. A dish well worth trying as this is Doomsday.

Blooms and balloons everywhere. Streamers and party hats. White confetti with black stick figures and dots on them gleaming in the artificial light. Real masks making funny faces.

This is it.

The childhood of the dead.

The hyperreal.

The world you hear about everywhere with its void of energy and sentiment. A world with no referent and no original and no private self. A world where images and signs and codes dump the real in Disneyland. A black hole of simulation and play-acting and mimicry which is here courtesy of McDonald.

And so Disneyland both provides illusion and prompts the desire for it. The simulation is now preferable to the real.

Right behind the door I can see a man seated at a dinky table with his hands around a paper cup. He is looking at the shape of a woman holding a solid mass in her arms. It is not a baby: too large and still. A toddler, perhaps, or the shape of a toddler petrified by the petrified look of parents in disbelief.

I can see a pretty little girl turning all red and ugly with tears.

— I would not have let you see her if I had known it would make you cry, says her mother.

— But I *wanted* to. I wanted to, replies the little girl. I just wish I had brought a hankie. I *wanted* to see.

And I can see her going into the slumber room with the two others. In front of the casket, she checks her father, drops her mother's hand, creeps forward and peeks at the body of her baby sister.

— But why did she die?

Her mother sings a lullaby in reply.

I can see a teenager with hands like spades burying his head in a mess of tenses. He used to surf like a god. But once he went off for a swim with his brother and came back alone. He banged and banged his head on the wall, then furiously mowed the grass in front of their house, and then the grass at the cemetery, day after day until the lawn turned into a muck coat for him to put on. Or so he used to say. They will use it tomorrow to cover the body of his brother instead, which is now all spongy and covered in creatures, and they will turn a blind eye to what this puny thing who begins every single sentence with *If only* says, said, or will ever dare say.

I can also see a woman like a mother with eyes fighting the shutters of forgetting: one is aching with the picture stuck in it, the other numb, drained, dead. On the picture in the right eye, there is a boy in a green outfit stretched out on an operating trolley, hair shaved, eyes turned back inside, and white, tongue lolling out of his mouth, thick and blue, his right arm hanging from the edge of the trolley, his left one stiff with thick liquid dripping into it—drip drip.

And the boy is slowly being wheeled well past the frame of the picture stuck in the woman's eye. Well beyond some history of original forgetting.

More than this, I cannot tell.

> *... but Disneyland tells us*
> *that faked nature*
> *corresponds much more to our daydream demands.[1]*

I go back the way I came, retracing my footsteps as it were, always hoping for some meaningful encounter.

The main entrance is not the way to go, I can tell you.

Dr Anon is still busy with mother. I like Anon although my father hates him: he was on duty the night I burned the bridge to the hyperreal. My mother is holding my baby sister in her arms. She is still very yellow.

— Breath-fed jaundiced, says Anon.

My mother turns green, the colour of fear, or guilt, or grief.

Memory. And now she looks as though she is the one who needs some drug or purge, for time has gone back to dark beginnings.

Just imagine, poisoned at the breast.

Dr Anon has read all that and he has fetched his book for her to read.

She *sees*, she says.

My big sister is eating raisins and dried mango, asking, *Will she die?*.

Farther is listening to the conversation next door, which has no door, but only a flimsy colourless curtain to draw open or shut between paper partitions.

Gita arrived from Punjab last week. It sounds as though she has malaria.

— I am very concerned and I strongly advise you to room in with her, says a lady doctor to Gita's mother who is not sure.

Gita will have her first birthday tomorrow. Only that you can be sure of.

Someone is opening the door to RESUSCITATION ROOM 1, which is lined with idiot sheets and tubes and vessels of all kinds. The table in the middle is but an ordinary table with a thin sheet of translucent paper on it. There are no intravenous nor I V equipment, no arm- nor footband extensions, no crutch sockets, no buckle-type body restraint straps. They lay a baby on the table and *stab him*—which is only doctor speak. They disappear behind a partition with the hypodermic needle and test tubes. They test the blood, then pour it down the drain.

Even here, or here more than anywhere else, things are provisional.

Out there to the West is the bridge I skip to when I am in time with the *twylight* just between night and dawn.

At this gate I always expect to see Peter with a key to hand over to me. But everyone knows that keys are useless here where you can worm through any w'hole at any time.

And so I climb up to the very top of the frame of the bridge and I sit on the brink of the world as you would know it.

From way up here I try to see past and far beyond the beginning of the real world. Past the factories and wharves, and past the greyness where ships skid by on the edge of the horizon. Past the chimneys puffing; through the air balloon taking off and beyond the point where the winds will push it towards. Past rings of smog like extinguishers on the wick of skyscrapers; inside and behind one, two, three planes with red eyes flashing, catching up with time, wrecking space.

Beyond the skies and the seas I can see birds like dustbins flying with scraps of plastic in their bills to unmake nests above bits of landscapes soldered together with black lead. To the West I know that there are monstrous yellow and red cranes with arms like claws tearing at the dirty mist.

But this I see for the first time: gigantic staves on ashen sheet music. A composition with no title. Just lines and spaces. Not here the notes, sharp, or flat, or natural, on lines and between them. Not here the treble clef, the key signature, the performance instruction, the time signature, the rehearsal marking, the rests and holds, the repeat signs. A set of lines folded back upon itself with ash *ad libitum*. A work with neither composer nor copyist.

But what of performers?
Since there are no breath marks there can be no singer.

So I look down on cars with lipstick yawning at the wheel or with eyeliner sticking to the wing mirror, and trucks with cigarettes fuming behind windscreens. Plenty of *Conformodores* with *phone-mobiles* too. Swish swish. All skating on this tombstone without an inscription, all sucked away, and down, into the mouth of some mythical beast ensconced in the palace of the racing gods.

But now I can see nothing, for I can hear *m*other singing to me. It is a recitative on a series of chords played on the harpsichord. It is clipped and grave and free in time, for the rhythm follows the sense of the words:

> Du haut de nos pensées vois les cités serviles
> **Comme des rocs fatals de l'esclavage humain...**[2]

Mother always sings with precision. So all I can see now is the partition in her mind with the breath marks firmly printed to indicate the brief pauses in her song.

m'other.

Way over where I can see, and sea, there is an eagle stamped with the mark of *twylight*. A mother eagle taking off, flying up, up. And now I can see her baby eagle all fluff and silk, a thing too young for flight feathers: the one that stole the eagle cloak.

The baby eagle sears through the twilight, back to the night.

The wind tears the coat and undercoat.

The eaglet falls in a nest of dusty down.

All gossamer and breeze.

The plumage of shooting stars.

A bunyip topples over a thick border of flaxen clouds, then down to the earth, and falls flat on the wet tarmac.

The laws of gravity are relative.

It is overcast, but well past dawn. I can hear a discordant note in the distance, as it moves by, step between two notes in harmony, and then a spinning out and unravelling of rhythm in a continuous pulsating movement.

O Welt, ich muss dich lassen.

I must find my way back to the *twylight* where stories are food, are aplenty, are strength.

---

[1] Thanks to Marco I have been able to use here the English translation of a text originally written and quoted in Italian: Umberto Eco, *Travels in Hyperreality* (London: Picador, 1987), p. 44. (Ed.)

[2] Alfred de Vigny, *La Maison du berger* in **Les Destinées.** The edition used here is unknown to me as mother only sings by heart. Further bibliographical referencing must therefore stop here, dear reader. (Ed.)

The Dance of Exile

Light and the ghostly water in the old glass
dissolved her bones.

Patrick White, *The Aunt's Story*

The day I broke Elsa's tower, she disappeared without even leaving a farewell note. And so I thought that perhaps she had realised at last that the time had come for her to end the history of a living lie.

For weeks I heard nothing of or about her. I tried to ring her at several of her old addresses and I rang a few of her old friends at whose house she was likely to have ensconced herself, for I was sure that she could not possibly have gone back home. All without any success.

One day, as I was putting away the things she had left at my place, it suddenly occurred to me that she might simply have cut off the cables of the telephone at Topsy-Turvy, for it had been dead for a while. So I packed a picnic lunch, just in case, and drove across a landscape of rolling plains to her house, asking myself why she had never called it home and why she had never talked to me about what it actually meant to her. She had, after all, been a keen designer.

When I got there, there was an auction sign with SOLD written diagonally across it, next to the gate, where *the ivy runs amuck*, as she used to say. Someone had mowed the lawn and a digger was busy scooping rocks and soil—a dam, I thought, and a good idea too, like taking down the tower whose panels now lay flat at the foot of the hill. Then I noticed a van parked right in the middle of the drive. I drove in and parked my car next to it. On the door on the side of the passenger was an inscription in red letters:

THE ASTRAL GLASS COMPANY

MANUFACTURERS AND SUPPLIERS
SPECIALIST IN
CUSTOM BUILT
GLASS HOUSES AND TUNNEL HOUSES
POLYTHEME SHADE HOUSES
POST-PARTUM CONSERVATORIES

Phoenix Ave, Killmore, Tel. 037/990011

Not bothering to reach for the picnic basket next to me, I got out of the car, slammed the door shut and walked up the alley to the back door.

I could hear a big fat rolling voice, like a lorry, pushing words together:

— Gotcha.

— No worries.

— No worries.

— Right-O.

Then a big fat belly laugh:

— No Wày Hosè !

— Beg your pardon, lady, what I'm trying t' say is that they don't work ... Anyway, if that's what ya want. But I can tell ya that I wouldn't want t' be doin' a root behind one of them one-way mirrors. Like I said: they don't work.

— Ah well, if that's what ya want, I'll sell one to ya. Then you can decide if ya want t' go ahead with the rest ... Now if

73

ya don't mind I'll go and get my sannies.

I thought that I'd best knock.

And who should open the door?

But Elsa.

Elsa wearing her death mask and ballet outfit.

I noticed immediately the necklace around her neck, a choker made of a gold chain threaded through three charms—tiny half grey stones—with a cavity lined with crystals—all hanging separately in the hollow of her throat, like ticks feeding on her breath. Her forehead looked even more protruding than before with her hair brushed back and tied high up in a tight knot. Her face looked whiter, and her eyes larger and greener, like split emeralds. Her body looked thinner too, much thinner, in fact, in her black leotard with long sleeves and black opaque tights. But her feet came as a surprise, as if drawing attention to themselves for the first time, in wild red slippers with silver drawstrings.

We did not speak.

She gestured me in.

Inside was a mess of papers and cardboard patterns and models and full ashtrays. There was also a still camera all smashed up and, amidst more papers, next to a wine glass and an empty bottle of WINDY HILL Pinot Noir, a film roll with its tongue torn and sprocket holes cut through.

Elsa noticed my reading the label on the bottle and confessed to having drunk *the whole thing* on her own—*very slowly though so as not to get sick*, the previous night.

At that, I understood that she was not begrudging me anything.

I moved some of the papers aside and sat down on the sofa. I could hear the contractor munching his sandwiches and grunting, but none of us seemed to take any offence.

— Look, said Elsa. I dreamed last night that this finger was cut right off, and look at this.

There was a bit of a cut, a bit of dried blood, even, but Elsa's index finger was still wholly whole.

So, I pointed to the ashtrays instead and suggested a pact: I would give up taking tranquillisers if she gave up smoking.

We called it quits and she showed me the plans of the greenhouse she wanted to build, or have built, since it looked a lot more complex than she had first thought.

The material used, to begin with, would not be plain old glass, nor polythene, but one way mirror stuff, which was tricky in itself. Then, of course, the shape would not be straight forward either: she wanted an octagonal greenhouse, to grow begonias in as well as 'produce vital beginnings', a phrase I did not understand, but I thought it was wise to ask no questions at this stage. The drawings themselves looked all right to me, except that there was no door, but I thought that perhaps this was another of Elsa's clever tricks, so I did not mention this either.

I was hungry and she was eager to get back to her scheme.

I only came back for a visit when all was completed. It was between Christmas and New Year, December 28th, in fact, early in the morning. I had brought some *panettone* and some *cougnou* for our breakfast, an espresso coffee-maker and fresh coffee beans, apricots, berries, and the last roses from my garden.

Where the tower had been there was now a huge octagonal hothouse partly framed by old rusty vines hung with tears. I thought of a bronze snare drum left out in the rain. I could see no door, so I walked across the wet lawn to the back door. It was open and I let myself in.

Elsa had not kept her promise, for the ashtray was full. She had tidied up though, and dusted, and swept, and put some fresh flowers in the vases: lots of forget-me-nots and daisies and handfuls of long grasses with drooping spikelets—wheat, rye and oats, plus some unidentified weeds. On the floor next to the bay window were three squares of proper tracing paper. The drawings looked like patterns of a tessellated floor for the greenhouse: the first one was the sketch of a tower after one of Bruegel's Babel paintings; the second was obviously unfinished, since it only had a few vertical lines on it, like streaks of rain, or sunshine, or moonlight; the third was a tree of life, with birds of different species perched randomly on its branches: an eagle, an owl, a bittern, a finch, a duck, a cuckoo, and a bird of paradise.

Elsa had tidied up her bedroom too. The typewriter had been put away, and so the desk was clear but for a bundle of letters tied with a green ribbon, a pot of black ink and a black fountain-pen. On the glass armchair next to the filing cabinet was also a pile of what looked like letters not sent. I could not resist the temptation: I sat down on the floor and read the one on the top.

Dear Hans,

Sorry for this long silence, but I have had to find my way back into my *m*other tongue. With a second-hand wheelchair and a new pair of artificial hands, this has taken a while, but here I am—you'll admit that my excuses are better than yours, won't you?

Anyway I've just come back from a holiday down The Great Mythic Sea Road. It was fantastic. The road itself pushes its way through the most rugged and spectacular landscape I have ever seen. A hundred miles or so from the City Post-Partum on the coast, the dunes slope between wild flowers, bushes, and volcanic stones to a green sea. From the road, it is as though you were following a thread back into history: high sheer cliffs on the surf, sharp white rocks reflecting on the waters, more bushes with spiky flowers, and slender gum trees with leaves like tongues and roots, desperately trying to hold on to the rocks. Every so often, the rough sea-coast shelters sandy inlets and that's also where you have to look for townships—or the odd petrol station.

Although it is said that the inhabitants of this land have rejected the idea of marketing the sky and the jagged contours of the shore, I wonder what it's going to be like when they have the Big Games in their Emerald City. But that's ages and miles away, anyway.

The other side of the bay is wonderful too, although, to tell you the truth, I only saw very little of it when I visited some friends whose parents live on the promontory the day I took a ferry to Wordsworth Point, just before taking the road for good and after *wetting my whistle* with Pat, who reminded me of your grand-father René.

That part of the coast opens right onto the sea. Rocky promontories contrast with tranquil inlets bordered with private properties and National Trust gardens. The most dramatic spots, I think, are around Wordsworth promontory: a wild, uneven coastline outlined by yellow and orange rocks, rocky reefs checking an unruly body of water and swift clouds that would make Coleridge cry his heart out. A mythical landscape after a true Dedalus' heart. Easy to imagine yourself as heir to Icarus here, or Ulysses—a figure much used in the literature of this country, by the way—did you know? Quite a contrast to your rooftops and chimney pots, don't you think?

Enough! I don't want to bore you with landscapes badly translated into words again. But, you see, I'm fine. Truly, I am.

Now what about you? Any more exciting or noble plans?

PLEASE do write.

Amitiés from the other one,

Elsa

P.S.: In a love affair most seek an eternal homeland. Others, but few, eternal voyaging. These latter are melancholics, for whom contact with mother earth is to be shunned. They seek the person who will keep far from them the homeland's sadness. To that person they remain faithful.... (Walter Benjamin, *One-Way Street and Other Writings*).

Fancy that. So that is where she was when I was madly phoning around. But the real question was where was she now?

Under this letter was a huge self-addressed envelope with a note from *Excellence Publishing* pinned to it—the rejection slip, no doubt. The black ledger inside the envelope could wait a while longer, I thought. She had, after all, given it to me the day I picked her up from The Tower and I had only bothered to leaf quickly through it. Perhaps that's why she took it back. Perhaps this is even why she ran away.

There was another letter underneath and I thought hard about whether I really should or not, but perhaps there was a clue.

                                        Easter No Matter When

Dear Hans,

Madness alone is truly terrifying, inasmuch as you cannot placate it either by threats, persuasion, or bribes. Don't worry, this is not a lecture on some universal decree, for you are the lawyer, but I can't help thinking about the fragmentation of old worlds at the moment, engrossed though I might be in my own Mirror World. Conrad is a great one to reread, anyway, when *one* is inclined to reflect upon things ethical.

Today the O.W. leader has been stabbed by a woman at a political rally in The City Vitrio. When he ended his speech, a woman in white came towards him. A bunch of flowers in one hand, a book in the other, she asked him for an auto-graph. When he leaned towards her, she stabbed him in the neck, then again in the back, killing him. The flower woman was arrested *sur le champ, mon brave*. When projectors lighted her face and the police asked her name, she just stood there and said 'I did not smother him'.

Well, you once said that you liked a good story. And this story is certainly snow-balling in many forms in the papers here. Strangely enough though, all agree to present the flower woman as The-Holy-Spirit-Itself. Not to be touched—the white dress?

But how are you anyway, and how is life far away from home? And when shall I get another one of your poignant and witty letters? Don't be too long or you'll get another of my mad ruminations.

Hoping to hear from you soon,
Best wishes and love,

Elsa Dedalus, your feather.

What a shame it would be now not to read the letter pinned to the envelope.

Excellence Publishing
P.O.Box 973 Mt Despair Vic 3790
Tel: (03) 793 1100

1 April 1996

Elsa D.
Topsy-Turvy
Cooe Muros
Land of Furphies 3034

Dear Elsa,

Please accept our apologies for not spelling out your full sur-name. I'm afraid that we are unable to decipher it on your submission.

We appreciate having had the opportunity to read your work. Although we cannot publish your submission, we sincerely thank you for your effort. We are sorry to disappoint you.

Please know that **Excellence Publishing** never rejects writers, only their writing, and that when we do this it seems to us that more work is needed before **Excellence Publishing** can consider publishing the work.

Unfortunately there is never sufficient time for the editor to provide any sort of comprehensive feedback to aspiring writers ordinarily submitting work.

If, however, you should require critical comment, we do offer such advice as separate service at very competitive prices. Manuscripts MUST be accompanied by a stamped, self-addressed envelope and cheques should be made payable to **Excellence Publishing**.

Yours most truly,

The Editor

The last sentence of the second paragraph had been crossed out in green ink, and in the margin Elsa had written in capital letters: AS IF ~~THIS MADE~~ THERE WAS ANY DIFFERENCE.

I then noticed something else on the desk: a syringe half-filled with black ink.

Oh, no, not that. That would be too kitsch.

And I walked out of the house, back towards the greenhouse where new answers to old questions must be.

Halfway there, perhaps, I heard a tap-tap and tap-tap and tap-tap, a continuous and obsessive tap-taping coming from the greenhouse. I thought that Elsa had given up dancing long before she came to this country, but what else could this be? I walked right up to the glass, for although I stood on the see through side of the one-way mirror I could not see inside because of the glare. I shaded my eyes with both hands and pressed my forehead against the pane.

There she was, skipping from one foot to the other.

She seemed to be looking at herself in the mirror though I could not see her reflection from where I was standing.

I moved slightly to the side. And then I both solved the mystery of the door and saw what Elsa saw: the door was cut in the same material as the body of the greenhouse, but it was curved back, and so Elsa in that mirror was like a long hair pin with huge red sticks for feet.

Just as I was going to turn back to the house to make some coffee and get the breakfast ready, Elsa moved to the centre of the concrete floor.

Boy, what a sight: an infinity of Elsa's leaping and bouncing and twirling around and around in an interminable pirouette, with arms lifted to the skies. Skies lit with both sun and moon, I saw, looking down upon this body, stretched like a string on the belly of a violin, with feet like painted nails now plucking all other invisible strings in frenzied pizzicati. A mock Bartok string quartet, she finished with a series of *chassé-croisés* in front of the panel next to the door and walked right up to the bronzed mirror to look at her face.

What she could see in the mirror I do not know. Perhaps she saw for the first time that the lines on her forehead were cracks. She looked closer and must have seen how broken it was inside. Had she seen through her frame? She looked frightened, and it looked as though the world was now whirling and twirling around, for she had to lie down. She must have remembered all the letters she had written telling tales of phoney friendships and funny hardships, a world of make-believe where she could have made it all happen.

Now was the time for me to go and make some coffee.

When I came back with a pot of coffee and an plateful of *panettone* and *cougnou*, the greenhouse was but a litter of glitter on the lawn. It must have exploded while I was grinding the coffee beans. Amidst the fragments and splinters and shards of glass was a pair of red ballet shoes with all ribbons knotted together. Nothing else that I could see.

Mother Worlds

Sun and shade are tricks
and I trust nothing
and I understand why we fear the telephone,
why, although we have cut the cables,
we still wait for the voice we dread;
and I understand mirrors
and try to track the point in their depth
when we become nothing - ...
Who owns us now?

Janet Frame, *Faces in the Water*

February 14th

I just woke up with a terrible headache.

Six, as usual, and the sunshine is already scorching my eyes.

Seven hours of sleep or so. Window half open, desk piled with books and cards and files, lamp still on. All as usual.

So why record all this *trivia*?

Damn, Hans's voice again. I'm sick of feeling as though I'm borrowing words all the time.

Ouch, my head!

And I haven't had a drop of alcohol in months. The thought of it alone makes me want to throw up.

The chirp-chirping of birds, the offended screech of a magpie, the distressed shriek of a cockatoo and the squawking and squealing of dogs on the chain. The chain scraping the concrete. A whistle high up in the sky. A ruffle of leaves. The neighbours must be back. Same noises as usual.

But wait.

One, two, three, four, five.

Not a peep from the factory on the other side.

Six, seven, eight, nine, ten.

I rip the cobwebs in my eyes to shreds that stick and I get up.
No, I don't. My head is full of lead and my belly full of sea-
weed. I must be coming down with something. Besides you
can't get up when you're writing. Oh, damn. Up, up, up or
I'll puke.

Now then.

I turn the radio on and try to listen to the news. Yesterday's
news, that is, as we get all the news from home which was
never home, a day, sometimes a week, later Down Under. I
wonder what news they get from here. Not that this makes
much difference. Well, not today anyway as there is no birthday to remember.

Coffee or tea?

'I'm in a quandary.' (Hans again.)

The white cockatoo is out on the verandah next door, so tea
it is. Not that tea's better for *mental cases*, dear Hans, but the
lonely like to put words around the emptiness of *trivialities*.
It's all in the mind anyway, as mother would have said.

Fortunately I have now let go of other silly rituals. But I can
remember those days at the flat in Little Firenze when I would
swap myself with a plastic doll to ease the pain. I must check
my diary of that year for details—though I doubt that I wrote
anything, but I remember clearly how I went out one Cup
Day to buy a human-size dummy, that looked like one of
those Madonnas Marco used to fall in love with in Rome, or
chase around the castle at Otranto, and how I used to lay it

down on my mattress once or twice each day of the week to make sure that I would at least move, if not get up, for a little while. I remember, for instance how I used to roll down the bed, with my clothes of the day before still on, struggle up onto my feet, throw the damned thing on the bed and get out every working-day of the week at 10 a.m. The tumble down the stairs, the race down the drive to the letter-box, and then, more often than not, the sob that would rise and never break inside my throat but on which I would choke. The shuffle back up the drive, the patter-patter up the stairs, the chuck of green bile in the toilet bowl, and finally the folding up onto myself in the white room where all was black.

Glasses now, for without glasses I'm not up to much these days. And I keep loosing them—*of course*. But never mind.

I must finish this desk-top with silver ash veneer and throw out the scraps of plywood. A clever design, this. Nice jigsaw of interlocking planes with all these recesses and shelves built into the cupboard. A desk to tidy up my life in.

I must also replace these Victorian panes with milk glass, come to think of it.

Now it's all much of a muchness out there if you ask me (*c'est du pareil au même si vous me demandez mon avis*), except that there is not one single car parked alongside the factory across the road. *Si vous voulez / tu veux mon avis* would be a better translation. Fancy that. It's coming back, my *m*other tongue.

But let's get out of here to see whether I'm here or there. For I, too, can pretend for a while that I belong with these bright young men who leave their beds at dawn to go and chase light after light in broad daylight, or those lovers tired of never loving, who skip across their beds at night to get away from inexplicable black thoughts and blue moods.

I must have missed or made up something, for here they all are: dozens of cars, underlining the fence between the factory and my place, and as many black sticks dotting the inside of the other world, dozens of dumb sentinels standing here frozen between the crumbled down tower and my downcast eyes.

And now I can see the smoke, and smell the stench of substances I've only read about, and I can also hear the hum and clunk and buzz of machines I would die to turn off every night as I switch off my computer.

But here I am in this world. The same world as yesterday's and tomorrow's. The same world as yours on the other side of the mirror, perhaps, although I cannot hear a word of what you are saying.

My sister is dead, and I must be until she is again inside my black outfit and behind my dark glasses and underneath my black hat.

Hang on, but how? With mother who is no more and no one to speak with.

Not the rope of time strung to time, but the rugged surface of space overlapping space, tugging at my moorings.

Perhaps I could do it if I now sat down with a book in my lap on one of those iron benches along a public garden whose play area is unfenced. The old recipes are the best, Chris used to say. And what if I now opened my book at a certain page starting with a paragraph underlined in green ink by some author who died in the midst of re-reading her book about unliving.

I take my (I)s off the page.

I turn the page.

No later than yesterday, she came and went as usual in a world that looked perfectly familiar to her.

Today she stands still and silent in a world that looks stranger and stranger to her every minute. A strange and estranging world which is slipping away, has slipped away. Not here the eyes that see, the ears that hear, the nostrils that smell, nor the hands that touch. Not here the sense of balance nor the common sense. A brand new world; perhaps not as unfamiliar as she fears though, for this is a world like a home, something one takes for granted, something credible yet incredible, true yet untrue, like a dream, a riddle, a story.

What else can she do but pinch her arm?

This world now looks to her the same as that other world far away beyond the seas and further than before days begone.

She takes a closer look.

And all in one glimpse she sees the rugged relief of the Borgium of her youth, its craggy and dull landscapes, the cacophony and discord and silence, the sweet and sour smells in the streets. She recognises the buildings and institutions, the political regime and the religions, the customs and mores and conventions, the cultural lore and the linguistic heritage, the legends and myths of an artificially created country for the sake of an artificial alliance. All of this she sees on one black and white print filed in a record out of reach on the only shelf in her memory that neither duster, nor vacuum cleaner, nor even index finger, has ever touched.

Dales and vales, plains and lakes, grasslands and freeways, skyscrapers and dens, towers and bowers, cathedrals and cemeteries, art galleries and prisons: a patchwork of words that do not fit well together.

She shuts her eyes to listen to the noise of engines roaring, wheels crunching gravel, feet clanking on the frosty tarmac; she tries to hear the chit-chat, of schoolboys and schoolgirls, the laughs of those who love, the sobs and yells of those who grieve, the screams of lonely men and women, the wails of babies, but all she hears is the sighing of words twirling down like snow flakes, and melting away into silence.

She puts her hands up onto her ears all the better to smell the fragrance of meadows and woodlands, the stench of cities and the stink of canals and ponds and lagoons, the scent of orchards and vegetable plots, the dusty smell of convents and presbyteries and school yards and ballet schools, the pungency of crowded ghettoes and slums and suburbs, the reek of rivers. The miasma of the living and the dead. But the essence of smells has drifted away and dried in the cradle of limp sentences that stay still.

And so with hands that are now scratching her head she reaches for more words—words like *monarchists* and *republicans, pacifists* and *neo-fascists, agnostics, protestants, muslims* and *catholics, anarchists.* With words like these she can see someone peering into a collection of poems, or translating the Bible, or reading the Koran; and there she sees someone else drowning a sister in green water, poisoning a mother, or smothering a baby, and further one other gouging a father's eyes, next to those in uniform who are throttling or burning alive their own kin to show to the world the root of all evil. All conceivable, acceptable, tolerable, commendable, or so it seems, in this kingdom of words that cannot hurt.

Thus this world cannot, must not, be the same as the other world. For her other world was but a series of variations on mutually exclusive themes invented by some one pompous, whilst this one is a multifarious representation of the one and only void parading as tolerance: a monstrous void beyond the borders of the law, an emptiness filled with words such as respect and acceptance and endurance and equal opportunity. A world with some pontificating other as head of state, a world with no real discipline, no restraint. Disorder with an order. A flawless make-believe.

Here she is in the midst of a swarming crowd, yet she is cold and hungry. Alone and lonely with all these faces swirling around. All befitting the real characters she imagines. She knows all of them, knows the faces and those hiding behind them, intimately, as though she has been with them ever since she was, as though she has lived through them, for them, against them, as though it was written that she should have loved and hated them since the very beginning. Yet all these characters are strange and hostile to her. It is as though they will forever look at her and not see her, yet see through her and turn their backs on her and shut their doors at the sound of her footsteps. A crowd crawling afar and apart. A crowd afeared.

No one looks at her.

No one speaks to her.

All too familiar, and so she eavesdrops.

What she hears in this now other world, is a mixture of dead and natural and modern and artificial languages, plain and private languages, good and bad language: a mixture of the various languages she had once learned, misremembered, and then unlearned. A bewildering babble and prattle she could not and cannot understand precisely because it does make sense.

Now, of course, she recognises the objects and artefacts and books around her and she could name all of them in both her mother and father tongues if only she could move her lips.

So, she must have known somehow that all these other worlds were one and the same with one difference, for she can read in her dictionary of the commonplace that appearances are not to be trusted, and further there is something about signifiers and signifieds not matching. But she knows about *multilingual thrush* and so she takes her eyes off the page.

The more she watches this brand new world, the more she thinks that all these things around her are reflections of other worlds she has seen on the flat surface of her no-time no-space. For all she can see now is a clutter of broken objects looked after by rejected children and broken children over-looked by spiteful grown ups.

All of a sudden she realises that she can no longer move. She is so heavy that she can see the thoughts in her mind knocking each other about. And no matter how hard she tries she still cannot move her lips. The thought of having at last found her own corpse in Borgium without having had to take notice of either the time or manner of her death is exhilarating. But she has to reject this possibility as she can see no bodies alight with fire and no dropping of ashes, nor is she swaddled in a shroud of darkness, and dirt inside a coffin inside a grave. Neither can she remember the clatter of the hearse nor recall the splatter of mud in her mouth.

But now she remembers having experienced such atrocious delight in other circumstances.

She can see herself seated in an armchair with a book in her lap and a puppy at her feet. She is seven or eight. She has her hair tied in a tight knot and her legs crossed like grown ups do. She lifts the book closer to her face so that other eyes can see the title on the dust-jacket: *Les petites filles modèles*. Her father looks at her from underneath eyebrows that gather in a twisting dagger. She smiles and then fades away.

She can see herself seated at her desk. She has a blue collar around her neck and a blue pen in her hand. Her lamp is not turned on and she squints in the twilight. She is transcribing a poem or a fable onto filing cards that she intends to ornament in the manner of medieval manuscripts. Her mother's cutting voice orders her off to bed.

She can see herself seated at an easel. She wears a butcher's apron which is far too large for her stunted frame and she holds a brush like a beak between her right index finger and thumb. She is copying a detail from a larger painting by Peter Bruegel the Elder reproduced on the cover of a book about translation, entitled *After Babel*, which is propped in front of the mirror of a dinky vanity table crowded with sheets and fragments of coloured glass, a glass cutter, breakers and grozing pliers, a soldering iron, cames, copper and silver foil, and bits of a broken chain.

She can see herself seated at the kitchen table. She has a white collar around her neck and a white pen in her hand. A candle is alight on a shrivelled up birthday cake that had grapes on it. Gold rimmed glasses sit on her nose. Her eyes are burning. She is translating a book, about exploring sun-bleached paddocks called grasslands, and looking at books that are like one-way mirrors.

Oh! The exultation and the lamentation of finding not a point of rest but new lines of flight. The abandonment of self to order in chaos. The utter relinquishment of voice and body and soul when she finds herself to be the sole onlooker in strange, familiar, and estranging, worlds, bound to a boundless unbounding no-time no-space.

Fear forsworn until the worms have eaten up all the words

and the silver fish all the paper until the rust has eaten away all the solder, soft or hard.

The face of death she has never seen, nor can she imagine ever seeing his shrouded back.

But what she can now see through the silver and gold in her field of vision is a white surface covered with glitter: a speculum, clamps and scalpels, tweezers and burettes, vacuum jars, culture tubes, a microscope and slides next to a garnet womb full of folds and holes and blotches around knots, the womb of her mother turned inside out on the immaculate marble of a dissecting table, waiting to be chucked down the throat of the incinerator.

And pulling herself off from the memory of deadness she starts to look for an exit in her mind.

She sits down. Gets up. Takes a few steps to the right; to the left. Sits down again, crossing her legs, uncrossing and stretching them, re-crossing them. Like Pinocchio she has to re-learn everything from scratch and she stumbles and trips and slips and strives again. Her body aches and her ache is taking away her memory, tracing the pattern of memories to come.

She can see herself seated in the doorway of a moonlit house. She will have no clothes on but a cloak made of feathers and he will be asleep in another room under the gaze of the wish star. She will stretch her legs into the sodden night and open a black notebook with a red spine and red corners on her thighs. She will take a deep breath. And she will sing. Then she will start writing about crossing worlds. And her words will swim. Then they will run away and fly and plunge in the wet moonlight. All *aswinging*.

She turns her ear inside and listens. She can hear some phenomenal bubbling and seething and rumbling inside herself. She listens to herself and her body tells her that hers is not the desire to travel towards this or that other world, nor to lose herself in the rift between them to bypass the present. Hers is the desire to live in and with the present and in the present tense, for she hears it and the time has come for her to disentangle herself from yesteryears and expand into tomorrows.

What she misunderstood in slumber, she now understands, for the real was as transparent as the wildest dreams of men and labours of wild women.

And what made no sense in her drowse she can now fathom, for the real unfolds and expands when dreams are conceived and labours get under way.

Thus the real of the Mirror World where she thought she had come alive was but the womb of an infinity of fabulous real worlds.

Whilst she listens to the sound of her own breathing, she hears the rhyming song of a secret being disclosed to her conscience. And so she now knows how futile it is for one to ask certain questions when one is not even certain that one can be.

And away from the fairies I turn the page again and I can feel the wish made flesh. There is now hope and joy ahoy, for what is now budding promise will be alive tomorrow: *a present*.

In memory of Elsa.
Esther, April 1st 1996

Epilogue

There then is the story of the elf woman who fed on feathers. You could piece it back together thus:

On the first day of the New Year, at the cross-roads of *m*other worlds on the edge of the Mirror World in the land of furphies, the woman who was mythtaken for an elf enamoured of wordsmiths found a pair of wings in the long green grass. She picked up the wings and plucked off all flight feathers and fine down. Then she ripped off the tightly meshed barbs from dozens of vanes and chopped them up. She also chopped and pounded the vanes and the quills to a silver powder.

When the sun dropped out of sight and sank deep into the sea, she tossed the feathers, all chopped to bits and covered in silver dust, into her mouth. She was hoping to have found how to grow wings at last, for she had heard of famous stories which all seemed to end in disaster, yet had thought herself wiser.

So she dreamed her way through

nine seconds of fancying

nine minutes of longing

nine months of imagining

until the brushing of crystals in her fat belly ceased to lift her spirits. A strange pounding pushed her own breath into her throat, onto her tongue and out rolled a groan from her lips.

She knew that the time had come for the great undreaming. She looked at the fat moon up in the skies and she saw in her field of vision the wish star twinkling next to Mercury. She now knew that she could look down at the many suns in the green sea without fear and she put her hands on her hips.

She walked and crouched and stamped her way through the gale in her body. She blew and breathed in, breathed out. Then she forgot all of her dreams and daydreams through what felt like the ending of the world.

Oh, no, my dear. Her insides were not ripped to shreds, nor her hips apart, by the mighty wings she had been growing.

She heard a short and fresh song. And so she knew that it was time for her to look down again, and ahead, far beyond the light and the ghostly waters.

She saw an elfish creature with a head the shape of a mango and a scrunched up berry for a nose, all smooth and waxy.

— The cord has stopped pulsating, said one bunyip.

SNAP.

— You are free, said she.

Then she took a deep breath and her second child was born.

It was then that her chest first tickled.

Her heart sneezed.

Most would have said or would still say that it was all a fluke of the spirits, some that it was a blessing, but the elf woman knew that *there* was her twin present from the gods.

It is October. The *m*other world is bursting with colours and words and the smell of wholemeal bread baking. And there comes the call of the bell bird as fresh and clear as the first note ever sung by an elf in love. On the vanity table is a bowl of grapes and a jug of clear water. The songs of new life linger in moon dust dancing in the morning sunshine.

Now, because of what I saw in the city post-partum, writes the mother, *I shall watch you like a hawk and call you Rinah and Zoë, for you are the singing and the breathing in my story.*

Other books by Dominique Hecq

Fiction

Mythfits - Four Uneasy Pieces
Magic & other stories

Poetry:

Good Grief
The Gaze of Silence

Short Drama:

One Eye Too Many